LIBRARIES
WITHDRAWN FROM

D0186125

By Jennifer Gray ★ Illustrated by

THE TRAVELS OF

Ermine

The Big London Treasure Hunt

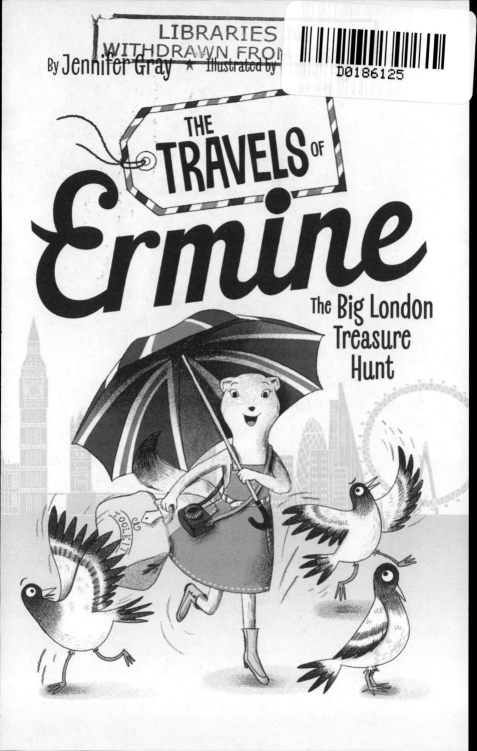

Dear Tom and Rani,

Thank you for your kind invitation to have Ermine to stay in London on her world travels. Since I adopted her, she has become very interested in history and wants to learn more about kings and queens, especially as Balaclavia doesn't have them any more.

I'm sure she will have a brilliant time with Minty – the two of them have so much in common!

With best wishes,

Maria Grand Duchess Maria Von Schnitzel

BALACLAVIA

OPEN LETTER

BALACLAVIA

Lord and Lady Lambchop

17 Mutton Lane

London

GB1 0LL

United Kingdom

Chapter 1

POLLY POTTER

The City of London...

It was the summer holidays and Minty Lambchop was up and dressed early.

She couldn't wait for their visitor to arrive.

Minty was eight years old. She had brown eyes and thick black curly hair tied into two even bunches. She had chosen her clothes carefully: a blue denim jumpsuit, white T-shirt and new trainers. She wanted to make a good impression.

POLLY Potter

Minty sat on her bed, staring out of the window expectantly. School holidays (especially summer ones) always *sounded* like a great idea, but now they were into week four and she was beginning to feel restless. Not that she wanted to go back to school yet – it was just that their house was a bit, well, CROWDED.

Despite being a lord and lady, Minty's parents – Tom and Rani – didn't have pots of money. The Lambchops' home was a tall topsy-turvy sort of house surrounded by other tall topsy-turvy houses in a narrow street in the heart of the old City of London.

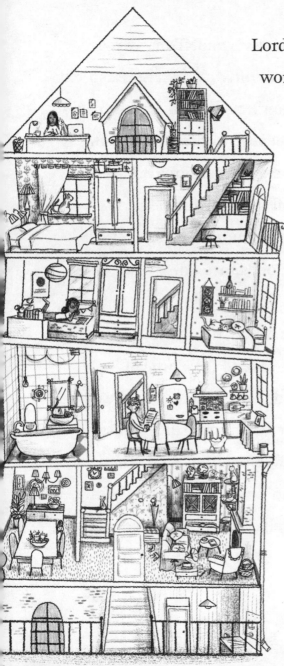

Lord Lambchop worked in the basement. Lady Lambchop worked in the attic. In between, there was a kitchen, a sitting room, three bedrooms and a bathroom, not to mention several flights of very steep stairs. And at the back was a tiny garden.

Minty's dad, Tom, was a conservationist. When he wasn't at home (like now), he was in far-off places exploring the deepest, darkest jungle. Big cats were Minty's dad's passion. But as he couldn't very well keep big jungle cats in a crowded London house, he kept domestic ones instead.

Minty's mum, Rani, was a children's author. She wrote books about a detective called Polly Potter and her trusty sidekick, Mable the talking parrot. When she wasn't writing, Minty's mum was reading. And when she wasn't reading, she and Minty helped Lord Lambchop look after his army of stray cats.

Minty loved reading too, especially detective stories. When she grew up, she wanted to be a famous sleuth and solve lots of mysteries, like Sherlock Holmes. She thought Polly Potter was **awesome**. She'd read all the **Polly Potter** books. She'd pinned **Polly Potter** posters on her bedroom walls. She had a **Polly Potter** duvet cover. She was even the proud owner of a limited edition **Polly Potter Detective Set**. The only thing she didn't have was a talking parrot.

But if what her mum had said was true, then she might be about to receive a visit from someone even better...

Just then, through the window, she spotted a black taxi appearing at the end of the little street. Minty jumped off her bed, flew down the stairs, and opened the front door.

The taxi drew up at the kerb. The driver got out and held open the passenger door. Out stepped a small, brown, furry animal with a long, bushy, black-tipped tail, two coal-black eyes, white whiskers and a pink nose. The creature was wearing a pinafore dress the same colour as Minty's jumpsuit and a mustard-yellow waterproof hat. A Polaroid camera was slung over one shoulder. In one paw it carried an umbrella and in the other a small bag marked TOOL KIT.

"Thank you," it said politely to the driver. Then it turned around and waved its umbrella at Minty.

"Hello," it said brightly. "I'm Ermine. You must be Minty."

Minty blinked. So it WAS true what her mum had said. Their visitor really *could* talk.

Move over Polly Potter and Mable, Minty thought, *here comes Minty Lambchop and Ermine, the talking stoat.*

Minty felt even more excited – they were going to have a **brilliant** time together, especially if they could find a mystery to solve!

"Ermine!" she cried. Ermine dashed up the front steps. The taxi driver trailed after her, carrying a very large number of very small suitcases, which he deposited in a pile.

14

Ermine placed the umbrella on the floor and removed her waterproof hat. "I brought these in case it rains," she said. "The Duchess said it *always* rains in London."

"It does rain *quite* a lot," Minty said carefully. She didn't like to tell their visitor that they were actually in the middle of a summer heatwave.

"We don't get much rain in Balaclavia," Ermine continued. (The Duchess had also told her that British people love talking about the weather.) "It's hot in the summer and it snows in the winter. That's when my fur changes colour from brown to white, so other animals can't see me."

"Awesome," said Minty. Being a master of disguise was an important part of detective work and it occurred to her that having a sidekick who could camouflage herself might prove very useful.

"Thank you," Ermine said. She gave a little sigh. "Although it didn't stop the Duke from trying to catch me."

"The Duke?" Minty echoed.

"The Duchess's husband," Ermine explained sadly. "He wanted to use my fur to trim his robes – the ones he used to wear in the old days when Balaclavia had a king. It's very precious, my fur. It's called ermine, like me. Luckily the Duchess came to the rescue. She told the Duke that the only place for ermine was on a stoat and adopted me instead."

"That *was* lucky," Minty, who was also adopted, agreed. The Duchess was right: the two of them really did have a lot in common.

They were going to be great friends.

Ermine nodded. "The Duchess taught me lots of useful things, like how to use a spanner and when to wear a feathered hat. And then she sent me on my world travels, so that I could meet new people and visit interesting places."

"That's a really good idea!" said Minty, thinking she'd like to do the same one day.

Ermine looked around anxiously. "Minty, do your mum and dad have robes?" she whispered.

"I don't *think* so," Minty whispered back. "They're not really that grand."

"How come?" Ermine sounded surprised. "They're a lord and lady, aren't they?"

"Yes, but that doesn't mean they're rich," said Minty. "Mum and Dad both work for a living." She explained what each of them did.

"You mean they don't get money from the Queen?" Ermine asked, puzzled.

Minty shook her head. "No. It doesn't work like that."

"What, not even in the old days?" Ermine insisted. It sounded very different from Balaclavia, where the King used to dish out money to all his favourites, like the Duke.

"Well, Dad's ancestor, Larkin Lambchop, *was* given some treasure, once upon a time," said Minty.

18

"So what happened to it?" said Ermine, looking around.

"It vanished," Minty said.

"Vanished?" repeated Ermine, intrigued.

"Yes," said Minty. "The mystery of the Lambchop treasure is one of the great unsolved crimes in British history."

Ermine's face set into a very determined expression. "Then *we* should find it, Minty!" she cried. "So your mum can write a book about it and your dad can put the money towards saving jungle cats." Her whiskers twitched in excitement. "And *we* can go down in history as the ones who finally solved the mystery."

Minty gave a whoop. "That's a **brilliant** idea, Ermine!" The lost treasure of the Lambchops was the *perfect* mystery for them to solve together.

Ermine clapped her paws together. *A treasure hunt!* It felt like the start of another **stoat-ily thrilling adventure!**

introducing

Minty Lambchop & Ermine

in The Mystery of the Lost Treasure

Chapter 2

At Ye Olde Tudor Cafe...

A little while later Ermine and Minty sat with Lady Lambchop around a small wooden table in a nearby cafe.

The cafe was in a ramshackle black-and-white building with stained-glass windows overlooking the River Thames. The cafe looked very old, especially compared to all the shiny new buildings surrounding it.

"It's been here since Elizabethan times," Lady Lambchop explained. Rani Lambchop

was a tall elegant woman with long dark hair, a ready smile and (Ermine thought) a daring choice of hat for the notoriously unpredictable British weather – a big straw one with a wide pink ribbon. Despite Ermine's concerns that it might rain, the sun was still shining brightly.

"And that's the Globe Theatre – where Shakespeare's plays are performed," said Lady

Lambchop, pointing through the open window.

The Globe Theatre also looked very old, like the cafe. It was round in shape, painted white on the outside, with thick dark wooden beams, tiny windows and a thatched roof. Ermine took a couple of snapshots with her camera to put in her scrapbook, while Minty told her mum about their plan to be detectives.

"A **treasure hunt?**" Lady Lambchop exclaimed. "What a good idea, Ermine!"

"Thank you," said Ermine distractedly. She was busy studying the menu on the blackboard.

Main course
Roast beef
& Yorkshire pudding
Fish and Chips
Pie and mash
Toad-in-the-hole
Bubble and squeak

Dessert
Bread-and-butter pudding
Jelly and ice cream
Iced buns

Ermine found the menu very confusing. She had never been anywhere where they ate pudding for a main course and bread and butter for dessert before.

But there was one thing on the menu that really puzzled her.

"Isn't that a bit yucky?" she asked, scratching her head.

"Isn't what a bit yucky?" said Minty.

"Toad," said Ermine. "Especially if you serve it in its own hole." She pulled a face, imagining a plateful of green toad served up on a bed of mud.

Minty giggled. "It's not a *real* toad, Ermine!" she said. "It's sausages in batter."

"*Toad* sausages?!" Ermine asked.

Minty giggled even more. "No! Ordinary sausages. It's got nothing to do with toads."

"Then why is it called toad-in-the-hole?" Ermine demanded hotly. How was she supposed to know that toad-in-the-hole was another name for a battered sausage?

Lady Lambchop came to the rescue. "I think it's called that because the sausages peep out of the batter, like toads peeping out of their holes," she said.

"Oh," said Ermine. She supposed that sort of made sense. Her eyes travelled back down the blackboard. "I didn't know you could eat bubbles and squeaks. What do they taste like?"

Minty laughed helplessly. "It's not *real* bubbles and squeaks," she said. "It's leftover cabbage and potato fried up together."

Ermine frowned. She wasn't sure she'd ever get the hang of British food. "What about the iced buns?" she asked. "Are they cold enough to make my fur turn white?"

"No!" said Minty. "They're not cold at all. The iced bit is just the sticky stuff on top."

"Why don't I order for you, Ermine?" suggested Lady Lambchop.

"I think that would be a very good idea." Ermine sighed.

The waiter came over. "Three fish and chips, please," said Lady Lambchop. She poured everyone a cup of tea from a large teapot. "Now, Ermine, if you're going to solve the mystery of the Lambchop treasure, you need to know the story of Larkin Lambchop," she said. "It's called the Great Pastry Plot."

The Great Pastry Plot. It sounded thrilling!

"Ooh, ooh, ooh," squeaked Ermine. "I love history." She cupped her chin in her paws and rested her elbows on the table.

"It all started back in 1565," said Lady Lambchop,

"when Elizabeth I was the Queen of England.
Elizabeth was one of a great dynasty of kings
and queens called the Tudors…"

Ermine listened hard.

"She was the daughter of King Henry VIII—"

"Wasn't he very large?" Ermine interrupted,
remembering a picture she'd seen
in her London guidebook.

"He was when he got
old," Minty told her.

"He probably ate too much bread and butter for pudding," said Ermine.

"Quite possibly," agreed Lady Lambchop.

QUEEN ELIZABETH I

"Anyway, after Henry died and Elizabeth became queen, she used to visit her father's old palace at Hampton Court. It's in a beautiful spot on the River Thames and Henry VIII built great kitchens there so he could entertain kings and queens from all over Europe…"

"Wait a minute, Mum. I need to write this down so we remember it all." Minty opened her **Polly Potter Detective Set** and took out a notebook and pen. She began to make notes.

"In those days, the Lambchop family worked in the kitchens," said Lady Lambchop. "The youngest of them, Larkin, turned the meat on the roasting spit. One day, when Queen Elizabeth was entertaining the French Ambassador, he noticed something very suspicious…"

Ermine felt a shiver run through her.

"While all the other cooks were taking the feast up to the Queen and her guests in the great gallery above, Larkin Lambchop saw one of the Queen's closest advisers – Lord William

Wellington – sneak through
the roasting kitchen and
pour poison in the
Queen's pie."

"No!" gasped Ermine.
Pouring poison in the
Queen's pie was a terrible
thing to do. "Why did he do that?"

"The Queen didn't have any children,"
Lady Lambchop explained. "Lord Wellington
thought that if he poisoned her, *he* could seize
the throne. But luckily Larkin Lambchop
raised the alarm just in time."

NO!
WAIT!

"What happened then?" asked Minty.

"The Queen was so angry with Lord William Wellington that she stripped him of his title on the spot, confiscated all his riches and ordered him to be imprisoned for treason," said Lady Lambchop. "And she was so grateful to Larkin Lambchop that she made *him* a lord instead and bestowed on him a priceless ruby from her very own crown."

Minty scribbled furiously.

"But the guards weren't paying attention," said Lady Lambchop. "Just as the Queen was handing Larkin Lambchop the ruby, Lord Wellington sprang from his captors and snatched it from Her Majesty's grasp. Somehow Wellington managed to escape. By the time he was recaptured the next day, the ruby had vanished."

Ermine was on the edge of her seat. It was one of the best stories she had ever heard.

"So, you see," said Lady Lambchop, "although the title has been passed down over the centuries through the Lambchop family, the whereabouts of the ruby remain a complete mystery…" She paused. "Although *some* say Wellington left a set of clues."

Clues! Minty put down her pen. She grinned at Ermine. This was definitely a job for Minty Lambchop and her trusty sidekick, Ermine!

Ermine grinned back. She couldn't wait to get going with *her* trusty sidekick, Minty!

Just then the waiter placed three platefuls of golden fish and chips in front of them. Ermine sniffed cautiously. To her relief, it smelled absolutely delicious. Maybe British food wasn't so bad after all!

She nibbled delicately on a piping-hot chip.

"There's only one thing for it," said Minty. "We need to find those clues, Ermine!"

"You could start at Hampton Court," Lady Lambchop suggested.

Hampton Court. Ermine chewed thoughtfully on a forkful of steaming white fish and crunchy batter. Her eyes fell on the river. "How about we take a boat?" she said.

Chapter 3

In some barracks near Buckingham Palace...

C orporal Bertram ("Beef") Wellington and his horse, Radish, had just finished a long morning on parade. Now they were back in the stable next to the barracks where the Queen's cavalry lived.

The Corporal sat on a small three-legged stool, polishing his boots. Radish stood next to him, tethered to his stall with his nose in a bag of hay. Corporal Wellington was still wearing part of his ceremonial uniform – white jodhpurs and a scarlet tunic with silver buttons. The rest of it lay on a rack beside him. He had already spent an hour polishing his silver helmet, breastplate and sword. But the thigh-length riding boots were by far the worst.

He regarded them gloomily. The boots glistened like coal. But glistening like coal wasn't good enough for Quartermaster Grouch. They had to twinkle like stars.

The stable door banged loudly. Footsteps pounded on the cobbles.

LEFT. RIGHT.
LEFT. RIGHT. LEFT. RIGHT.

Beef Wellington gave a deep sigh.

Talk of the devil…

Quartermaster Grouch marched over and lunged towards him. "**GIVE IT SOME WELLY, WELLINGTON!**" he shouted. (Quartermaster Grouch always shouted, even when his mouth was a centimetre away from your ear.)

Beef Wellington's eardrums vibrated painfully. But it didn't do to disobey Quartermaster Grouch. The Quartermaster had all manner of cruel and unusual punishments for soldiers who disobeyed his orders.

"Yes, sir!" he said meekly, buffing the boots furiously.

"HOW MANY TIMES DO I HAVE TO TELL YOU? THOSE BOOTS SHOULD BE TWINKLING LIKE STARS, NOT GLISTENING LIKE COAL!" bellowed Quartermaster Grouch.

"Yes, sir!"

Quartermaster Grouch stood up. He took a long, hard look at Radish's gleaming flank. "And when you're done with that you can groom your horse properly. It's got dust on its coat."

"But..." Beef Wellington clamped his mouth shut. He'd been about to point out to the Quartermaster that it was impossible for a large, jet-black horse to stand in a stable full of sawdust without getting dust on its coat, before he realized his mistake.

But it was too late.

Quartermaster Grouch's throat began to rumble like an erupting volcano.

Beef Wellington braced himself. He was in for it now!

DID I HEAR YOU SAY *BUT?*

the Quartermaster roared.

"No, sir!" Beef Wellington lied.

Quartermaster Grouch's face was scarlet, like his tunic. **"BECAUSE IF I DID, LADDIE, YOU'RE FOR THE CHOP. THERE'LL BE NO SNAKES AND LADDERS AFTER TEA FOR <u>YOU</u> TONIGHT."** (No snakes and ladders after tea was one of the Quartermaster's favourite cruel and unusual punishments.) **"GOT THAT, WELLINGTON?"**

"Got it, sir."

The Quartermaster clicked his heels, marched back along the cobbles

LEFT. RIGHT. LEFT. RIGHT.

LEFT. RIGHT.

and slammed the stable door.

Beef Wellington glared daggers after him. It was bad enough not being allowed to play snakes and ladders after tea with the rest of the regiment, but it was the use of the word "chop" that really enraged him.

"Chop!" he muttered, grinding his teeth.

"Chop!" he choked, rolling the word around his mouth and spitting it out like a bad banana.

"Chop, chop, *chop,* CHOP, CHOP!" His voice rose to a scream.

Radish stopped chewing and wriggled his nose out of the nosebag. He whinnied.

Beef Wellington pummelled his boots with the polishing cloth. "I should be the one giving orders and dishing out cruel and unusual punishments around here, not Quartermaster Grouch," he fumed. "And that's not all…"

Radish drew his lips back from his teeth and made an ugly face. He knew what was coming.

"I shouldn't be a corporal – I should be a lord! *Lord* Bertram 'Beef' Wellington: Head of the Household Cavalry, Knight of the Garter, Great Master of the Most Honourable Order of the Bathtub, Leader of the Noble Society of Silk Socks, Guardian of the Queen's Chamber Pot,

Chief Taster of Royal Pies, Collector in Residence of the Queen's Toenail Clippings..."

Corporal Beef Wellington reeled off a great long list of things he ought to be in charge of.

Radish snorted impatiently. He'd heard it all before.

"It's *true*, Radish," his keeper insisted. "Us Wellingtons have a proud history. I've been doing some more research online – look." Beef Wellington pulled a piece of paper from his pocket and spread it out on his knee.

Radish eyed it hungrily.

"It's not food, Radish, it's family," Beef Wellington said crossly.

THE LORD WELLINGTONS

of Britain

WILLARD THE WELLINGTON
(founder of the Wellington dynasty)
1066 – 1123

LORD WILBERFORCE WELLINGTON
(the stupid) 1237 – 1301

LORD WINSTON WELLINGTON
(the wise) 1169 – 1237

WALLACE WELLINGTON
(the brave) 1123 – 1169

LORD WALTER WELLINGTON
(the old) 1412 - 1513

LORD WILLIAM WELLINGTON
(THE TRAITOR) 1515 - 1565

LORD WOEBEGONE WELLINGTON
(the hopeless) 1360 - 1412

LORD LARKIN LAMBCHOP
(the noble)

LORD WISHFUL WELLINGTON
(the hopeful) 1301 - 1360

LORD WALTER WELLINGTON
(the young) 1513 - 1515

And his descendants (1565 to present day)

Beef Wellington brandished the piece of paper at Radish. "If it wasn't for that **loathsome** busybody, Larkin Lambchop, William Wellington wouldn't have been declared a **traitor**. AND if William Wellington hadn't been declared a traitor, I'd still be a lord and have tons of money and a big castle."

Radish shook his mane.

"I know, I know, Radish, all William Wellington's riches were seized. But he escaped with the Queen's ruby, remember?" Beef Wellington narrowed his eyes. "If **only** I knew where to find that jewel, Radish! It's rightfully **mine!** I shouldn't have to spend the rest of my life polishing boots until they twinkle."

Radish lifted his tail. A steaming pile of manure plopped onto the sawdust.

"I agree with you, Radish," growled Beef Wellington. "It STINKS. The only good thing is that those lousy Lambchops never got hold of the jewel either." He thrust his feet into the polished boots and stood up. He'd come to a decision.

"You know what, Radish?" he said. "Once a Wellington, always a Wellington. Quartermaster Grouch can stuff his snakes and ladders. I'm going to find my ruby. And no one – not even Quartermaster Grouch – is going to stop me." He gathered the rest of his uniform, picked his way carefully through the sawdust, untied Radish and led him out of the stables. Then he jumped on his back.

Radish pricked up his ears. He pawed the ground eagerly.

Beef Wellington's face had set into a determined expression.

Chapter 4

That afternoon on the River Thames...

Ermine sat on the top deck of the boat with Minty and Lady Lambchop, taking snapshots with her Polaroid. The boat was called *The Jolly Jester* and was one of several paddle boats that sailed up and down the Thames, showing tourists the sights.

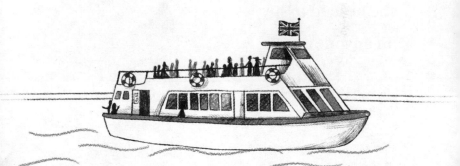

Ermine was still wearing her blue pinafore dress but, on the advice of Minty, had exchanged her waterproof hat for a deerstalker. According to Minty, a famous sleuth called Sherlock Holmes always wore a deerstalker hat and Minty had been very excited to find one on an old doll that was just the right size for Ermine. Ermine was delighted at the thought that it made her look like a proper detective, even if it was a bit tickly around the ears.

Ermine wasn't the only one dressed like a detective. Minty was wearing a sunhat and dark glasses (just in case she needed to spy on anyone)

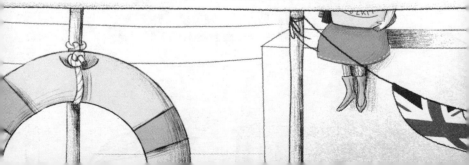

and had brought along her **Polly Potter Detective Set** to decipher clues.

The Jolly Jester puttered gently along the river in the bright sunshine. It had been a very good idea of hers to take the boat, Ermine decided. It was the **perfect** way to see London!

Old Royal Naval College

London
Eye

RIVER
THAME

ELEPHONE

Houses of
Parliament

Big Be

Richmond

Richmond Park

Tower of London

Globe Theatre

OXO Tower

Tate Modern

Westminster Abbey

Lambeth Palace

RIVER THAMES

Battersea Power Station

Now the boat was meandering past the picturesque town of Richmond, on their way to Hampton Court. With its grand houses and green lawns, Ermine thought it was one of the loveliest places she had ever seen.

"In Tudor times, the kings and queens used to travel by barge along the Thames between their palaces," Lady Lambchop told her. "Although London looked very different then!"

Ermine tried to imagine London as it was 450 years ago, without all the tall buildings and cars and red buses and people. She consulted her guidebook to see if there were any pictures. But she spotted something else instead.

She gasped. "Is it true that Henry VIII had *six* wives?" she demanded.

"Yes, it's true!" Minty said. She had just

been learning about the Tudors at school.

"All at the same time?" Ermine asked, aghast.

Minty pulled a face. "Yuck! No! One after another."

"How come?" asked Ermine.

"Haven't you heard the saying?" Minty replied.

Ermine shook her head. "What saying?"

"Divorced, beheaded, died; divorced, beheaded, survived," said Minty.

DIVORCED: Catherine of Aragon

BEHEADED: Anne Boleyn

DIED: Jane Seymour

DIVORCED: Anne of Cleves

BEHEADED: Catherine Howard

SURVIVED: Catherine Parr

"Beheaded?!" squeaked Ermine.

Minty nodded. "The King got fed up with his first five wives because they didn't give him a son," she explained. "Except the third one, who he loved, but she died. The last one outlived him."

Ermine stroked her whiskers thoughtfully. "Why did Henry VIII want a son so much?" she asked.

"It was tradition," Minty explained. "When the King or Queen of England died, their sons inherited the throne ahead of any daughters."

Ermine looked indignant. "What, even if the boy was a *baby*?" she said.

"That's right," Minty said.

"But you can't be a king if you're a baby!" Ermine spluttered. "You'd be rubbish at it.

And anyway, it's not fair – girls are just as good at ruling as boys."

"Of course they are," said Minty, "but they didn't think like that then. And Mum was right: in the end the throne *did* pass to Henry VIII's daughter, Elizabeth, and she became a great queen."

"Ha! That proves it then," said Ermine. What silly ideas some humans had about things!

She returned to her guidebook. "Is this her?" Ermine pointed to a picture. It showed a stern lady with a white face and red hair, wearing a splendid dress and a heavy crown encrusted with precious gems.

"Yes, that's her," said Minty. "She's the one who gave the jewel to Larkin Lambchop."

Minty removed her magnifying glass from the Polly Potter Detective Set. The two of them used it to study the picture carefully. At the front of the Queen's crown was a big, fat, red ruby. "Ermine! Look!" cried Minty. "I think that might be the Lambchop ruby!"

But something else had caught Ermine's attention. "Wait a minute," she said in a horrified tone, "is that *fur* on the Queen's collar?"

Queen Elizabeth I

Fortunately at that moment they rounded a bend in the river and Hampton Court Palace came into view. It was a magnificent building of soft red brick. Either side of the stone entrance stood two great turrets. Behind them, huge chimneys rose into the sky.

Ermine dropped her guidebook and scampered across the deck of the boat to get a better view. "**Ooh, ooh, ooh!**" she squealed in delight. Now they were actually at the palace, she had no trouble imagining what life was like in Tudor times. She felt like Queen Elizabeth I arriving at her royal abode!

The boat docked. Ermine collected her tool kit while Minty shoved the guidebook in her pocket and grabbed the **Detective Set**. The two of them stepped off the gangplank with Lady Lambchop.

"I'll go and explore the gardens while you two investigate," said Lady Lambchop. "See you back here in two hours. Good luck!" She waved goodbye.

Minty pulled her sun hat down over her

ears. "Let's start in the kitchens," she said to Ermine. "And we'd better make sure no one's following us."

"Why would they be?" said Ermine.

"Who knows?" said Minty mysteriously. "But you can never be too careful when you're a detective."

She led the way through the stone entrance and across a cobbled courtyard. Ermine scampered behind. This was their chance to make history!

CLIP CLOP, CLIP CLOP, CLIP CLOP!

The sound of hooves on the stones made Ermine turn her head.

A **HUGE** black horse trotted across the courtyard. On its back rode a soldier, dressed in a scarlet tunic, white jodhpurs and long black boots.

On his head he wore a plumed silver helmet, and tucked into his belt was a long silver sword.

The horse came to a halt. The soldier dismounted and tethered it to a post. "Stay here," he told the horse.

The horse snorted.

"Pssst! Minty!" Ermine hissed.

Minty stopped and turned. "What?"

"Why is there a horse in the courtyard? And who's that man? You don't think *he's* following us, do you?

He does look a little suspicious."

Minty looked at the horse and rider from under her hat. Then she shrugged. "You don't need to worry about *him*, Ermine. He's one of the royal guards. This way!" Minty disappeared through a door.

Ermine followed her into a smaller courtyard crowded with barrels and carts. They entered a building called the Boiling House.

"I don't know about Boiling *House*," grumbled Ermine from under the deerstalker, "but it's boiling *hot*!"

They passed through the Boiling House along a narrow street and into the main kitchens. Ermine couldn't believe how many buildings there were. Hampton Court was more like a village than a palace.

Inside the Great Kitchen it was even hotter. A huge fire roared in the grate, like in Tudor times. To one side of the fireplace a man dressed in Tudor costume slowly turned a haunch of meat on a spit.

Ermine whipped off her deerstalker and

began to fan her ears with it. "Minty! Look! That must be where Larkin Lambchop was when he spotted William Wellington poisoning the Queen's pie!" she squealed. She hurried over to where the Tudor man sat.

Minty hurried after her.

"I'm Ermine Stoat," Ermine said importantly, "and this is my assistant, Minty."

"What?" cried Minty. "But you're supposed to be *my* assistant!"

Ermine frowned. "I'm the one with the special hat, remember?" She turned back to the man. "We're detectives. We're here to solve the mystery of the missing Lambchop ruby."

There was a great clatter behind them.

CRASH!

Ermine and Minty looked round. To Ermine's surprise, the soldier in the red tunic sat in a heap on the floor beside a table, surrounded by fallen pots and pans.

Ermine scurried over and fanned him with her hat. "Are you all right?" she said.

The soldier stared back at her, open-mouthed. He looked as if he'd had a terrible shock.

"He must have fainted from the heat," said Minty. "He needs water."

"Leave it to me." Ermine shinned up the table leg and grabbed an old stone flask. She pulled the stopper out with her teeth and poured the contents over the soldier's head.

"That's not water – it's mead!" cried the Tudor man.

Ermine didn't know what mead was, but

from its gluey consistency, the sickly smell
and the number of flies buzzing round
the soldier's hair, it was made
from something sweet
and sticky.

"It's a Tudor drink made from honey," Minty whispered.

"Oh," said Ermine. That explained the flies. "Sorry about that," she said to the soldier, while the Tudor man handed him a glass of water and helped him to a chair.

The soldier still seemed in a daze. Minty was right, thought Ermine, the heat must have got to him. Either that or he'd seen a ghost. An old place like Hampton Court must be full of them. She returned to the fireplace with Minty and the Tudor man.

"You know all about the Great Pastry Plot then?" said the Tudor man.

Minty and Ermine nodded solemnly. "We intend to find out where Lord Wellington hid the Queen's ruby," said Minty.

"It belongs to Minty's family, you see," explained Ermine. "She's a Lambchop. Her mum's going to write a **Polly Potter** book about it and her dad's going to use the money to save jungle cats. And we're going to make history by finding it."

There was another clatter.

CRASH!

Ermine looked round. Now the soldier had fallen off his chair!

People fussed around him.

What on earth was the matter with him now? wondered Ermine.

"Do *you* know where we can find some clues?" Minty asked the Tudor man.

"Maybe." The Tudor man scratched his beard. "Have you heard the old rhyme?" he said.

Ermine and Minty shook their heads.

"It goes like this," said the Tudor man.

Cock-a-doodle-doo,
a plot began to brew.
Wellington poisoned the pie,
left the Queen to die,
But Lambchop knew what to do.
Concerned for her safety,
He shouted, *"THE PASTRY!"*
But William escaped
down the loo.

Minty wrote it
in her Polly Potter
notebook. "So that's
how he escaped! I
didn't even know they
had loos in those days."

"Me neither," said
Ermine. "I thought people
went in the woods, like weasels."

"Not at court," said the Tudor
man. "Here – I'll show you."

He led the way out of the kitchens and up
the stairs to an enormous gallery lined with
tapestries. Ermine sat on Minty's shoulder,
clutching her tool kit. She gazed in awe at
the beautiful wooden ceiling.

"That's where Elizabeth I was sitting

when it happened." The Tudor man pointed to a great throne at the far end of the gallery. "And this is where Wellington made his escape." He led them past the throne into a small room. Inside the room, tucked discreetly into the wall behind a tapestry, was an ancient loo. Ermine peered down it cautiously, one paw placed delicately over her nose, just in case.

"It's called a garderobe," said the Tudor man. "And don't

worry – it's clean. No one's used it for a few hundred years."

"Where does it come out?" Ermine asked.

"The river," the Tudor man said. "William Wellington climbed down it, jumped on a passing barge and made his getaway. Though he was probably a bit **smelly** by that point."

"Do you think he might have left a clue *in the loo*?" Minty wondered.

"There's only one way to find out," said Ermine in a determined voice. "Hold this!" She rammed the deerstalker hat into Minty's hand. Then she scampered down Minty's jumpsuit to the floor, opened her tool kit and took out a rope and a head torch.

"Here!" She tied one end of the rope to Minty's ankle and the other end around her waist using a strong knot, strapped the head torch firmly around her ears, jumped into the hole and abseiled down the loo.

It all happened so quickly that Minty and the Tudor man barely had time to blink!

Minty leaned over the shaft. She cupped her hands round her mouth so she could shout down.

"ARE YOU OKAY, ERMINE?"

"OF COURSE I'M OKAY!" came a squeaky echo from somewhere far below. "I THINK I'VE FOUND SOMETHING! WAIT, I'LL TAKE A PHOTO."

POOF!

Ermine's camera flashed.

POOF!

It flashed again.

There was a tug on the rope. "PULL ME UP!" Ermine ordered.

Minty placed both hands on the rope and pulled.

After a moment, Ermine came into view. She leaped out of the hole straight into Minty's pocket.

"Can I see the pictures?" Minty said.

"Not here," whispered Ermine. "They're top secret. And it was you who said there might be someone following us, remember!" She looked about furtively. "Let's go somewhere private and I'll show you. Can you think of anywhere?"

Minty's eyes lit up. "How about the maze?" she said.

Chapter 5

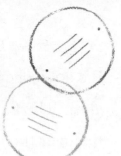

A little while later,
at the Hampton Court maze...

C orporal Beef Wellington hid behind a large stone statue near the entrance of the maze. Radish stood beside him, pulling clumps of lush grass from the lawn with his big teeth and chewing them noisily.

CHOMP, CHOMP, CHOMP!

"I'm telling you, Radish, it could talk!" Beef Wellington swiped at a bee. His hair was still sticky from the mead and his red tunic was stained an unpleasant treacly brown.

Radish snorted.

"It *could*, Radish! It's a **stoat detective**. It's got a deerstalker hat and a magnifying glass. The Lambchops must have hired it to uncover the mystery of what happened to the Queen's ruby." He swiped at another bee.

Radish tore off an even bigger clump of grass and chewed that too. Galloping all the way from the barracks to Hampton Court was hungry work for a big horse.

CHOMP, CHOMP, CHOMP!

Beef Wellington elbowed his steed in the ribs. "Will you **stop** stuffing your face and listen to me, Radish? It's a detective. A particularly sneaky one, if you ask me. And it's after MY treasure. It found a **CLUE** in the **loo!**" He swiped at a third bee. The beastly things were everywhere.

Radish's head jerked up. The horse looked at its owner questioningly.

"Yes, *that* loo – the one William Wellington escaped down in 1565," said Beef Wellington. "The stoat abseiled down it and took a photo of something. And before you ask how I know, I was hiding behind the tapestry outside the garderobe.

"That's why we're here. So we can spy on it again – it might lead us to the ruby." He pulled Radish's reins.

"*Shhh!* Look, there it is! Over there with the girl."

Ermine and Minty were approaching the maze. Ermine had resumed her place on Minty's shoulder, her deerstalker hat pulled down firmly over her ears.

"Two tickets, please," Ermine said to the attendant in a loud, clear voice.

"*See?*" Beef Wellington hissed. Radish clacked his teeth in astonishment.

"Can I interest you in a joint ticket for the apiary?" the attendant asked Ermine.

"What's that?" asked Ermine.

"The royal beehives," said the attendant.

"They're just over there." He pointed to a group of small wooden huts tucked away under some trees.

"Is that where you get the honey for the mead?" asked Ermine with interest. "Only I just spilled some by accident in the kitchen."

"That's right," said the attendant. He chuckled and lowered his voice. "But don't tell the bees!" he whispered. "They don't much like having their honey taken."

"I don't blame them," Ermine whispered back. "We stoats don't much like having our fur taken."

Beef Wellington strained to hear. *What were they whispering about? Was it something to do with bees?*

"I'll let you into a little secret," murmured

the attendant. "There's only one thing bees hate more than having their honey taken – and that's something eating their foxgloves."

Beef Wellington couldn't quite catch it. *Foxes? What did foxes have to do with bees?* He shook his head crossly. He wished they'd speak up.

"Thanks for the tip," said Minty in a normal voice. "We'll just do the maze today."

The attendant handed her the tickets. "Don't get lost!" he said cheerily.

"Don't worry, stoats have an excellent sense of direction!" Ermine replied.

"They're ermazing at mazes," Minty giggled.

The two of them disappeared inside amid peals of laughter.

"Come on, Radish," Beef Wellington hissed,

swatting at another bee. He took hold of the horse's bridle. "We'll go the other way. Then we can spy on them when they get to the middle." He and Radish waited until the attendant's back was turned and tiptoed through the exit gate.

Beef and Radish hurried along the narrow passage between the tall hedges until they came to a fork in the path.

"This way!" Beef Wellington said, leading Radish to the left.

On they went between the tall hedges until they came to another fork in the path.

"This way!" Beef
Wellington said, leading
Radish to the right.

On they went again.

"Curses!" said Beef
Wellington. They'd
reached a dead end.

"Have a look and see where
we are, will you, Radish?"

Radish reared up on his
hind legs and peeped over the
hedge, only to see Ermine
and Minty hurrying by in
the opposite direction.

He waved a hoof to show
his owner which way
they'd gone.

"Back, back!" said Beef Wellington. He felt very hot and flustered. The syrupy mead was sticking to him like glue. It was all that meddling stoat's fault! Beef Wellington had a good mind to let Radish trample it. More and more bees buzzed around his ears and tunic.

They got to a fork in the path. "This way!" Beef Wellington said, leading Radish to the right.

On they went between the hedges until they came to another fork in the path.

"This way!" Beef Wellington said, leading Radish to the left.

On they went again.

"Curses!" said Beef Wellington. They were back where they'd started!

BZZZZZZZZZZZZZZZ...
ZZZZZZZZZZZZZZ...
BZZZZZZZZZZ!

And the bothersome bees were gathering
in number. They seemed to be attracted to
the mead.

"We'll just have to cheat," Beef Wellington
said crossly. He leaped on to Radish's back
and bent low in the saddle like a racing jockey.

"Tally-ho, Radish!"

Radish cantered along the path between the hedges, closely pursued by the bees. This time, whenever they reached a dead end, instead of trying to find another way round, Radish jumped over it.

A few jumps later, Beef Wellington drew the horse to a halt. He could hear voices. They were almost at the middle of the maze!

Beef Wellington peered
cautiously over the hedge.
Minty and Ermine sat on a bench
in a small clearing surrounded by tall
foxgloves. The two of them were poring
over a Polaroid picture with
Minty's magnifying glass.

The clue in the loo!

Ha ha! Beef Wellington smiled to himself. Stoats and Lambchops weren't the only ones who could play detective! It was his family treasure, and he was going to be the one to find it! He took out a small brass telescope from his tunic pocket. The telescope was a family heirloom – one of the few things passed down through generations of the Wellington family after they were stripped of their wealth. He put the telescope to his eye and twisted the barrel until the photograph came into focus.

Beef Wellington found himself squinting at a picture of what looked very much like ancient graffiti. He gasped. William Wellington the Traitor must have scrawled it on the garderobe during his escape so that his family would be able to find the jewel if he was ever caught!

Beef Wellington read it carefully. Or at least he tried to.

> The ruby is mine. None shall know.
> Now on to the Archbishop's Garden I go.
>
> (Lord) William Wellington 1565

Beef Wellington scratched his head. It didn't make any sense!

Just then Minty carefully removed something from a slim briefcase and handed it to Ermine. Beef Wellington zoomed in with the telescope to get a better look.

He barely had time to register that the object in Ermine's paws was a compact mirror when she opened it.

BOOF!

The sun's rays reflected
off the mirror onto the
telescope lens, down the
barrel and straight into
Beef Wellington's eye.
The glare was so bright
it nearly made him
fall off Radish.

Beef Wellington clutched his head in agony. His temples throbbed. He could feel his headache worsening.

Painfully he steadied himself and forced his eyes open to take another look.

Now Ermine was holding the photograph up to the mirror, while Minty jotted something down in a notebook.

Beef Wellington frowned. What on earth were they doing?

Suddenly the penny dropped. The clue in the loo was in mirror writing! The letters were reversed. If you saw it in a mirror, you could read it.

He raised the telescope cautiously and zoomed in on the notebook.

> The ruby is mine. None shall know.
> Now on to the Archbishop's Garden I go.

(Lord) William Wellington 1565

A wicked smile spread across Beef Wellington's face. *The Archbishop's Garden.* He knew exactly where that was!

He pocketed the telescope and ducked down behind the hedge. Ermine and Minty were getting ready to go, but Beef wasn't worried about them any more. He had this treasure hunt in the bag! All he had to do was make sure he got to the ruby before they did.

He waited until they'd disappeared, then dug his heels into Radish's flanks. "*Tally-ho, Radish!*" he hissed.

But Radish didn't budge. Instead, Beef

Wellington felt a strong tug on the reins.

YANK!

While Beef Wellington had been spying on Minty and Ermine, Radish had been doing some spying of his own.

FOXGLOVES!

Radish stretched his powerful neck over the hedge and lunged at the luscious flowers. He tore off a big clump and began to chew.

CHOMP CHOMP CHOMP.

Then he tore off another big clump and chewed that too.

CHOMP CHOMP CHOMP.

Beef Wellington looked around in alarm. An angry buzzing was coming from close behind them.

BZZZZZZZZZ!
BZZZZZZZZZ!

The bees!

But the bees weren't just bothersome any more. They were positively **scary**.

A great cloud of them had formed above Radish's tail.

Beef Wellington gulped.

"YOU STUPID HORSE!" he cried.
"LOOK WHAT YOU'VE DONE."

Radish stopped
mid-chomp. He
swished his tail
angrily at the bees.

BZZZZZZZZZZZZ!
BZZZZZZZZZZZZZZZZZZ!

The bees ignored
him. One of them flew down
and stung Radish hard on his rump.
Radish let out a squeal. He bucked and reared.
Beef Wellington clung to the saddle.
"STOP IT, RADISH!" he shouted.

But Radish wasn't
listening. All of a sudden, he bolted.

Ermine and Minty had reached the
exit of the maze.

"LOOK OUT!" cried Minty.

The two of them crouched down as a large
black horse bearing the red-
coated cavalry soldier
sailed over their heads
and thundered across
the gardens towards
the River Thames,

closely pursued by a
swarm of bees.

There was a loud

SPLASH.

"Oh dear," said Ermine. "I hope
they can swim."

Chapter 6

The next morning at 17 Mutton Lane

Ermine and Minty sat at the breakfast table in their pyjamas, surrounded by Lord Lambchop's cats and puzzling over the clue in the loo. Minty's pyjamas were covered in cats, like the kitchen. Ermine's were an eye-catching shade of pink.

The ruby is mine. None shall know.
Now on to the Archbishop's Garden I go.

Ermine's London guidebook was propped
up against the teapot. She leafed through it
briskly while Minty looked up *Archbishop's
Garden* on her mum's tablet.

"We're looking for *Tudor* gardens,
remember?" Minty said, helping herself to
some cereal.

Ermine nodded sagely. She'd already gone
through the guidebook and flagged all the
Tudor landmarks with
Post-its, on Minty's
instructions.

She dunked a toast soldier in her boiled egg, and turned to the next page. "Ooh, ooh, ooh!" she squeaked through a mouthful of eggy toast. "This must be it!"

LAMBETH PALACE and GARDENS

Lambeth Palace was built in 1435. It is the London residence of the Archbishop of Canterbury.

"Brilliant!" said Minty. She put her spoon down and typed the name into the tablet. "Here it is." She clicked on a website.

Ermine dabbed egg yolk off her whiskers with a napkin. "It says in the guidebook it's closed to the public," she said disappointedly.

"Not today it isn't," Minty said as she scrolled down. "Look!" She turned the tablet screen so that Ermine could see.

Lambeth Palace Garden

EVENTS

Lambeth PALACE GARDENS FETE

SATURDAY 30TH JULY
LAMBETH PALACE GARDENS
12.30 P.M. TO 5 P.M.
including

FACE PAINTING   DOG SHOW
LIVE MUSIC   TOMBOLA
STALLS   TUG OF WAR
CREAM TEAS   RAFFLE

"I'll ask Mum if we can go."

Ermine clapped her paws in excitement.
A garden fete! She'd never been to one before,
but the Duchess had told her they were so
popular in Britain that even the Queen had
one every summer. Ermine couldn't wait to
taste the cream tea and try her paw at the
tombola. Suddenly a thought struck her.
"Minty, is the Archbishop very important?"
she asked.

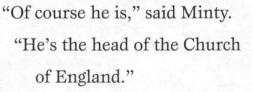

"Of course he is," said Minty.
"He's the head of the Church
of England."

Ermine snapped the
guidebook shut. "Then
I shall need to wear my
feathered hat," she said.

This time, instead of taking the boat, Lady Lambchop, Minty and Ermine travelled to their destination on the Tube. Ermine didn't like the Tube nearly as much – it was very noisy, packed with people and far too squashy, but she had to admit it was a lot quicker.

Very soon they arrived
at Lambeth. The palace
looked like a mini version
of Hampton Court. The
fete was being held in
the gardens.

Ermine sat on Minty's shoulder as
they entered the grounds through a side gate.

"Family ticket with free entry to the raffle?"
the lady in the entrance booth asked.

"I'm not really family," Ermine said a
little sadly.

"Of course you are!" the lady replied
cheerfully. "We're ALL part of a family in
Lambeth. We like to think of ourselves as one
big community."

That made Ermine feel so warm and happy

inside she had to stop and take
photos with everyone to put in her
scrapbook to show the Duchess, including
ones with the Lambeth schools jazz band
and the Kennington Tandoori tug-of-war
team, who arrived at
the same time.

"I'm going to the book stall," said Lady Lambchop. "Remember to keep your eyes open for clues!" She waved goodbye.

"Let's make a note of our observations," said Ermine to Minty.

"Good idea," Minty agreed.

Ermine perched on Minty's shoulder while Minty went to work with her notebook and pencil.

The first thing they saw was the ice-cream van.

The second
thing they saw
was the dogs
and their owners
practising for the
dog show.

The third thing they saw was the soldier
and horse they'd seen at Hampton Court.
Traces of dried mud lingered on the soldier's
boots, and the horse had a big lump on its
rump. It gave Ermine
a dirty look,
as if it wanted
to eat her
feathered hat.

Ermine jammed the hat firmly onto her head. "What's *he* doing here?" she whispered to Minty. "It seems very suspicious that he keeps turning up everywhere."

"I've told you, Ermine, you don't need to worry about him," said Minty. "He's probably guarding the Archbishop or something. Besides, if he was spying on us, he'd be incognito."

"In *what*?" asked Ermine.

"Incognito! It means he'd conceal his identity. Let's go."

Ermine looked at the horse again. Now it seemed to be sneering at her. Its lips were going all wobbly. She frowned. The soldier and his horse might not be spying on them, but there was definitely something funny going on.

They climbed some steps up to a gravel walkway. On the other side of the walkway more steps led down to a wide lawn crowded with stalls and people. Children chased each other in circles around the grass.

"What's that?" Ermine said, pointing to a stone plinth beneath an arch of roses further along the walkway. The plinth looked very old, as if it had been there since at *least* Tudor times.

"It's a sundial," said Minty, going over to look at it.

Ermine was mystified. "What's a sundial?" she asked.

"It's an ancient way of telling the time," said Minty, who'd learned about sundials at school. She placed Ermine on the sundial so she could see better.

113

The dial was like a clock face with Roman numerals, the number twelve at the top.

"The lines and numbers represent each hour of the day," Minty explained to Ermine. "When the sun shines, you can tell the time from where the triangle's shadow falls."

Ermine was fascinated. "That's really clever!" she said. Then she frowned. "What happens if it's cloudy?"

"I don't know," Minty admitted.

"Do you think the sundial might be a clue?" asked Ermine.

"Maybe," said Minty. She took out her magnifying glass from her Polly Potter Detective Set and examined the dial. "Wait a minute," she said. "Look at this."

In the middle of the sundial, just beneath the triangle, someone had scratched a message in tiny letters:

8, 1, 2, 2, 5, 10
WW woz here!
1565

"The sundial must be a decoder ring!" said Minty.

"What's a decoder ring?" Ermine asked. It sounded very mysterious.

"It's a way of sending secret messages," Minty told her. "I've got one in my Detective Set." She took it out and showed it to Ermine.

"Each number represents a letter," Minty explained.

"All we have to do is work out which letters match the numbers, then we've cracked the clue."

"You mean the numbers spell a *word*?" Ermine squeaked. This detective stuff was **thrilling**.

"Precisely," said Minty.

Ermine clapped her paws together. **"Ooh, ooh, ooh!** I **LOVE** puzzles! I do them all the time in Balaclavia with the Duchess!"

Minty began to sketch the dial in her notebook. "I don't get it," she said after a while. "The alphabet has twenty-six letters but the sundial only has twelve numbers. How are we supposed to work out which one represents what?"

"*Shhh!*" said Ermine. "I'm thinking."

She counted something on her toes. "**Wait!** I think I know! The numbers on the dial go up and down from 12. Maybe the letters do the same." She plucked the pen from Minty's grasp and jotted them down in the notebook.

"So what does it say?" asked Minty breathlessly.

Ermine copied the secret message into the notebook:

8, 1, 2, 2, 5, 10

Then she wrote the matching letters underneath:

W, A, B, B, E, Y

"Wabbey?" said Minty. "What's a wabbey?"

The two of them exchanged mystified glances.

"Wait! I think I know!" said Ermine. She pulled out her London guidebook from Minty's pocket and opened it to a yellow Post-it.

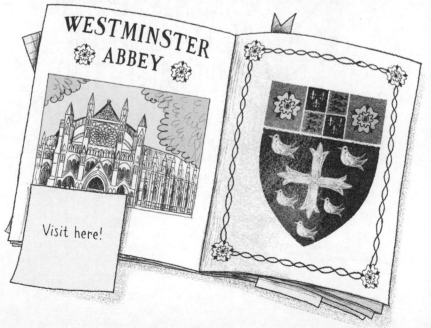

It was one of the places she'd looked up that morning.

"Westminster Abbey!" exclaimed Minty. "Of course! Ermine, you're a **GENIUS!**"

"Well, maybe *not* a genius…" began Ermine modestly.

Just then a voice came over the tannoy:

WOULD MISS ERMINE STOAT PLEASE REPORT TO THE RAFFLE TENT WHERE THE ARCHBISHOP IS WAITING TO PRESENT HER PRIZE.

"Woohoo, Ermine!" cried Minty. "You won a prize! Let's go and get it. Then we can play Splat the Rat." She snapped her notebook shut.

Ermine straightened her feathered hat. This really was turning out to be the

BEST DAY <u>EVER!</u>

Chapter 7

The next day at the barracks...

Beef Wellington was having a **HORRIBLE** morning.

5 **a.m.** parade practice was pants...
6 **a.m.** breakfast was beastly...
7 **a.m.** mucking out was manky...
And 8 **a.m.** running was rotten.

Now he was back in the stables, polishing Radish's hooves. It seemed like everything was going wrong. The mead. The bees. The river. And to top it all, Lambeth Palace was only open to the public one day a year. He'd had to go along to the garden fete just like everyone else. And guess who'd arrived just ahead of him…

"I HATE that smarty-pants weasel detective and her little friend," said Beef Wellington bitterly.

Radish snorted in agreement.

"I mean, it's bad enough them going after my treasure, but winning a raffle prize as well – that's just plain unfair."

Beef Wellington had never won a raffle prize in his life, let alone met an archbishop. In fact, he'd never won anything – not even an egg-and-spoon race. He ground his teeth at the injustice of it all. "Well, one thing's for sure, Radish – that weasel's not getting its paws on the Wellington ruby." He stood up and gave Radish a sugar lump. "Luckily I had my telescope with me," he grumbled, "although they've even managed to ruin *that*!"

Beef Wellington withdrew the telescope from his tunic and regarded it crossly. He'd tried to sneak up on Minty and Ermine at the fete, with the result that the telescope had been crushed by Minty's wonky aim with the hammer at the Splat the Rat game.

It looked more like a periscope than a telescope now. But it *had* come in handy for spying round corners when Minty and Ermine were watching the dog show...

"Westminster Abbey," he said thoughtfully. "I wonder if the treasure's actually *hidden* there, or if there's another clue..." He scratched Radish fondly between the ears. "Well, we'll soon find out, Radish. Once we escape from Quartermaster Grouch..."

The stable door banged.

"It's him!" Beef Wellington hissed. "Leave it to me, Radish. I'll do the talking."

Quartermaster Grouch marched over. LEFT. RIGHT. LEFT. RIGHT. LEFT. RIGHT.

"WHAT COLOUR DO YOU CALL **THOSE, WELLINGTON?**" he shouted, pointing at the mud-stained boots.

"Green, sir," said Beef Wellington.

"*GREEN?????!!!!!*" yelled the Quartermaster. "**THEY SHOULD BE TWINKLING LIKE STARS, <u>NOT</u> GREEN LIKE WELLINGTONS, WELLINGTON!**"

"Yes, sir."

"**AND WHAT'S *THAT* ON YOUR TUNIC?**" Quartermaster Grouch demanded, eyeing the brown patches with disgust.

"It's mead, sir."

"*MEAD?????*" Quartermaster Grouch roared.

Beef Wellington nodded.

"**THIS ISN'T A TUDOR PICNIC, WELLINGTON!**"

shouted the Quartermaster.

"No, sir!"

"YOU'RE **NOT** HENRY VIII."

"Definitely not, sir."

"YOU'RE A MEMBER OF THE HOUSEHOLD CAVALRY, WELLINGTON. YOU SHOULDN'T BE DRINKING MEAD."

"I *didn't* drink it, sir," said Beef Wellington. "A talking weasel poured it over my head in the kitchens at Hampton Court Palace."

The Quartermaster looked as if he might explode.

A TALKING WEASEL???!!! THAT PROVES IT, WELLINGTON. **YOU'RE BARMY!** GO AND HAVE A COLD BATH...

(Having a cold bath was another one of the Quartermaster's cruel and unusual punishments.) **"AND TAKE YOUR HORSE WITH YOU.**

IT'S GOT A **LUMP** ON ITS **RUMP**
THE SIZE OF A **CAMEL'S HUMP!**"

"Yes, sir," said Beef Wellington meekly.
**"AND NO JAMMIE DODGERS
FOR A WEEK!**" (That was another.)

Quartermaster Grouch marched out of
the stables.

LEFT. RIGHT. LEFT. RIGHT.
LEFT. RIGHT.

Beef Wellington leaped off the stool.
He had no intention of having a cold bath,
especially not with Radish.

"Tally-ho, Radish," he said. "Next stop
– Westminster Abbey! We need to get there
before that repulsive weasel and her Lambchop
friend, so we can find the next clue before they
do and get back the Wellington jewel."

They cantered out
of the barracks...

past Buckingham Palace...

through St James's Park...

and into
Parliament Square.

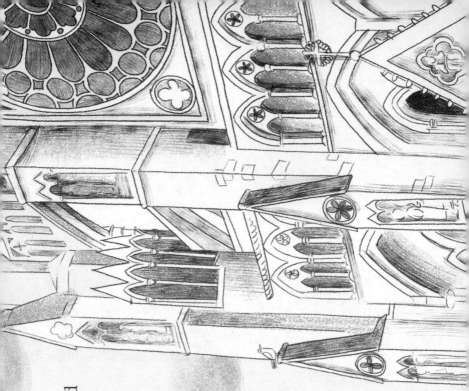

A few minutes later they arrived outside Westminster Abbey – just in time to see the great wooden doors open and Minty and Ermine disappear inside.

"CURSES!" cried Beef Wellington. "They're here already!" He quickly dismounted. "Wait here, Radish."

Radish shook his head and pawed at the ground.

Beef Wellington
relented. "Oh all right, Radish,
you can come with me. But if
anyone sees you, freeze.
They'll think you're a statue.
You got that?"

Radish whinnied.

They crept
through the
great door.

"Look! There they are!" hissed Beef Wellington.

Ermine and Minty had joined a tour group. The two of them were listening avidly to the guide.

Radish shook his mane at seeing Ermine again. His rump was still *very* sore.

"Come on, Radish – the guide might have some clues!"

Beef Wellington and Radish hurried along the aisle, keeping to the side. Luckily for them, the abbey was so echoey that no one noticed the sound of Radish's hooves CLIP-CLOPPING on the tiled floor.

They stopped a little way away from the group. Beef Wellington listened closely.

"Most visitors enter the Abbey through the

134

north transept," said the guide. "Their first
impression is of the soaring height of the vaulted
ceiling. At 102 feet, it is the highest in England."

The group looked up in awe, including
Ermine, who was sitting on Minty's shoulder,
wearing her detective hat and taking notes in
her scrapbook.

"Get on with it!" muttered Beef Wellington. He couldn't care less about the vaulted ceiling. Wellingtons weren't known for their climbing – he was sure there wouldn't be any clues up there.

"The rose window above the entrance is one of the finest stained-glass windows in the world," said the guide.

Everyone looked.

No clues there either, thought Beef Wellington fretfully, chewing his fingernails.

"The north transept also contains several larger-than-life statues of early prime ministers…"

Beef Wellington suddenly realized that the guide was pointing towards him and Radish.

"Freeze, Radish!" he hissed, ducking down in the nick of time behind an early prime minister.

Radish froze.

"And…er…one of their horses," said the guide.

The group moved off.

Once they were sure no one was looking, Beef Wellington and Radish hurried along the aisle to catch up with them. This time they hid behind a coffin.

"Thirty-nine monarchs have been crowned in Westminster Abbey," said the guide. "They have all been crowned sitting in the Coronation Chair."

"Was Elizabeth I crowned in the Coronation Chair?" Minty asked.

"Yes." The guide nodded.

"It's a bit scruffy," observed Ermine doubtfully. The Coronation Chair wasn't nearly as grand as she had expected. It was more like the sort of thing you'd find at a car boot sale.

Beef Wellington tried to get a look
with his telescope.

He could see what she meant. The chair
was covered in graffiti.

"Most of the graffiti was carved many years ago by pupils from nearby Westminster School," explained the guide. "They used to sneak into the Abbey during the night and leave messages."

"What about the rest of the messages?" Minty asked. "Is there anything about treasure?"

"Well, there's this one," said the guide. He pointed at one of the carvings.

Beef Wellington and Radish exchanged feverish glances.

Ermine and Minty squinted at the chair. Then Minty opened the Polly Potter Detective Set and took out a piece of tracing paper and a pencil. She held the paper against the carving while Ermine got to work.

"They're making a rubbing, Radish!"

whispered Beef Wellington. "It must be a clue!"

He zoomed in with the telescope.

I'VE TRICKED YOU ALL, YOU SILLY FOOLS
I'VE STUCK IT IN THE CROWN JEWELS!
KINGS AND QUEENS FORGET ME NOT
THE LEADER OF THE PASTRY PLOT!

WW 1565

Beef Wellington blinked. *Of course!*

The Crown Jewels!

No wonder the Wellington treasure had
remained hidden for so long. What better
place to hide the Queen's ruby than with
other royal gems?

The Tower of London. It was the last place anyone would think to look!

Beef Wellington's face broke into a joyful grin. If they hurried, he and Radish would be there before the Lambchop girl and the weasel. Nothing could stop him now! The ruby was almost in his grasp. William Wellington would be proud of him.

Just imagine, thought Beef dreamily as he tiptoed out of the Abbey with Radish, *if the Great Pastry Plot had actually succeeded.* William Wellington would have become King of England. He'd have had all the jewels he wanted – not just one ruby…

Suddenly Beef had a brainwave. The thought of his devious ancestor had given him the most **fantastic idea**. *Why not steal all the Crown Jewels while he was there?* They practically belonged to him anyway. Or they should do. He, Beef, might not become king (well, not yet, anyway) but he could still be richer than any Wellington had ever been! He could buy an island, or five, and live there with Radish for the rest of his life in a big castle. They would eat caviar and sugar lumps and watch movies all day, while sharks swam around the moat, keeping out weasels.

And he would **never** have to see small, furry, brown detectives, Lambchops or Quartermaster Grouch EVER **again**.

Beef Wellington gave an evil chuckle. Talk about history. It was time to go out all buns blazing. The Great Pastry Plot was about to rise again. He leaped onto his horse's back. **"Tally-ho, Radish! To the Tower!"**

They galloped off in the direction of the Tower of London.

Chapter 8

Closing time at the Tower of London...

Ermine and Minty had also worked out the clue.

"So that's where the ruby is!" said Lady Lambchop as they jumped in a black taxi. "No wonder no one has ever found it until now!"

"I should have realized!" said Minty. "It's called hiding in plain sight – when you hide something somewhere so obvious that no one thinks to look there."

Hiding in plain sight. Ermine made a mental note of it for the future. It was clearly something all good detectives should know.

Very soon they had arrived at the Tower of London.

The Tower was the most imposing of all the Tudor landmarks Ermine had yet seen. The massive stone turrets loomed high above her as dark storm clouds gathered in the sky.

They hurried across the moat to the portcullis. A man stepped out from behind the iron grille. He was dressed in a bright-red uniform: red stockings, a frilly collar and a broad-brimmed hat adorned with fluffy bobbles. In one arm he carried a vicious-looking pike.

"Who's *he?*" Ermine whispered to Minty in alarm.

"He's a Yeoman of the Guard," Minty told her. "They're also called beefeaters."

How odd, thought Ermine. But then most things about London were a little bit odd. It must have to do with its history – a history that Ermine still very much intended to be a part of!

"HALT! Who goes there?" said the beefeater.

Ermine took charge. "I do," she said. "And so does my friend Minty, and her mum, Lady Lambchop."

"Lambchop, you say?" said the beefeater. "As in LARKIN LAMBCHOP?"

Ermine nodded. "We've been investigating the mystery of the Great Pastry Plot—" she began.

"We know where William Wellington put the Lambchop treasure—" Minty interrupted.

"It's hidden in the Crown Jewels," Ermine interrupted back. She wished Minty would behave more like a sidekick sometimes. She really would have to have a word with her about it if they were ever to solve any more mysteries together.

The beefeater whistled. "You'd better come in." He raised the portcullis. "My name's Greville, by the way."

Just then hooves pounded on the cobbles. They turned around.

A great black horse with a lump on its rump the size of a camel's hump galloped across the drawbridge towards them. On its back was a soldier dressed in a stained red tunic and dirty boots. He was brandishing a wonky telescope and had a crazy look in his eye.

The horse gave a loud snort. It pulled a horrible face at Ermine as it shot past.

"Them again!" said Ermine. She turned to Minty. "Who do you think he's guarding *this* time, Minty? Only, I think they might be following us."

"He's not guarding anyone," confirmed the beefeater. "That's been the beefeaters' job at the Tower since Tudor times."

"So what's he *really* doing here?" said Minty.

"I don't know," said Ermine. "But something tells me we'd better find out."

The little group chased after the horse and rider.

"LET'S TAKE THE SHORTCUT!" shouted the beefeater, diving left under a low archway.

The Tower was a bit like Hampton Court, Ermine realized. Inside it were streets, buildings and grassy squares, most of which seemed to have very gruesome names. Ermine caught sight of two of them as they rushed along, which was enough to tell her that she didn't want to see any more.

THE BLOODY TOWER

THE SCAFFOLD SITE

There was also a pen containing some large black birds with vicious-looking beaks.

She hurried past with a shiver.

In a little while they arrived outside the Jewel House.

Ermine gazed up at it. The Jewel House was like a castle all by itself. It had thick, stone walls and a pair of big black gates, with the words

written above them in huge gold letters. One of the gates was open.

From inside the Jewel House there came a **SMASH**, followed by the shrill scream of a burglar alarm.

BRRRRRRRRRRRRRRRRRR!

"I had a feeling that man was up to no good!" said Ermine.

"HE'S STEALING THE CROWN JEWELS!" cried Minty.

"We've got to stop him!" said Ermine in a determined voice. "Come on!"

"I'LL CALL FOR HELP!" cried the beefeater. He and Lady Lambchop raced off.

Minty and Ermine crept into the Jewel House. The heavy metal door guarding the vault where the Crown Jewels were kept was open. They peeped around it. Inside the vault they could see a walkway lined with glass cabinets full of precious treasure.

SMASH! CRASH!

Ermine gasped. The soldier and his horse were working their way along the cabinets. The horse was **smashing** each glass panel with a well-aimed kick of its powerful back legs. The soldier followed after it, pulling things out of the cabinets and stuffing them into a nosebag.

"*What are we going to do?*" whispered Minty in dismay.

Ermine cast her eyes along the display cabinets. At the very end was one containing a mannequin of Elizabeth I. The mannequin was clothed in a **magnificent** velvet dress. In one hand it held a sceptre, in the other hand an orb. And on its head was a crown encrusted with jewels – the most gorgeous of which was a glittering, red ruby.

She gave Minty's hair a tug. "Minty, look! That's IT! The LAMBCHOP RUBY!"

CLANK! CRASH! THUMP!

The soldier and his horse made their way towards it, throwing things into the nosebag.

The soldier was muttering William
Wellington's final message under his breath:

"I'VE TRICKED YOU ALL, YOU SILLY FOOLS
I'VE STUCK IT IN THE CROWN JEWELS!
KINGS AND QUEENS FORGET ME NOT
THE LEADER OF THE PASTRY PLOT!"

"He's gone **mad!**" whispered Minty.

It was true, thought Ermine. The soldier
had a reckless look about him. Not to mention
his dirty appearance. That dip in the river at
Hampton Court hadn't done the trick – he
looked as if his uniform could do with a
good wash.

Suddenly she had a **brilliant idea.**
"Minty, do you still have that prize I won at
the garden fete?" she whispered.

Minty nodded. "It's in my backpack. Why?"

Ermine whispered something else, very quietly, in Minty's ear.

Minty's face lit up. "Great thinking," she hissed. "I'm in!" She high-fived Ermine's outstretched paw.

Ermine collected her TOOL KIT from Minty's pocket and set off at a run. She scampered along the floor to the back of the last display cabinet.

Quick as a flash, she opened the TOOL KIT and removed a hairpin and four tiny suction pads.

Taking the hairpin in her mouth, she placed a pad in each of her paws and squirmed up the glass to the lock. Ermine inserted the pin. She twiddled it carefully with her teeth.

CLICK!

It only took a few seconds for the lock to give.

Ermine let go of the suction pads and dropped to the base of the cabinet. Then she pulled open the glass door as far as she could so that Radish wouldn't kick it. Finally she **scurried** up the back of the mannequin's magnificent dress and draped herself across the neckline, in a **perfect** imitation of an ermine collar. *Phew!* she thought to herself. *Just in time! This hiding-in-plain-sight thing had better work!*

Beef Wellington and Radish were approaching.

"**HA HA, RADISH!**" cried Beef Wellington.

"HERE IT IS AT LAST! THE WELLINGTON FAMILY JEWEL!"

He reached forward and plucked the ruby from the crown.

"NOT SO FAST!" cried Ermine, uncurling herself from the mannequin's neck. Beef Wellington and Radish boggled at her. They both looked terrified, as if they thought the mannequin might suddenly come to life too!

Seizing her chance, Ermine sprang forwards, snatching the ruby from the astonished soldier's grasp.

Clasping the jewel in her teeth, Ermine raced back towards the exit.

Radish gave an angry neigh.

Beef Wellington recovered himself.

"IT'S THAT PESTILENT WEASEL DETECTIVE AGAIN!" he shouted, mounting the horse. **"QUICK, RADISH! AFTER IT! WE WELLINGTONS DON'T GIVE UP THAT EASILY."**

So that's it! thought Ermine as she scampered along. *The soldier is a descendent of William Wellington.* No wonder he'd been following them. He'd been trying to work out the clues so he could find the ruby his ancestor had hidden!

She dashed towards the door of the vault.

"DON'T WORRY, ERMINE, I'VE GOT THEM COVERED!" Minty shouted. "NO ONE GETS PAST MINTY LAMBCHOP, ESPECIALLY NOT A WELLINGTON." She reached into her backpack and took out Ermine's raffle prize.

BUBBLICIOUS – THE WORLD'S BUBBLIEST BUBBLE BATH

Minty opened the door of the vault.

Ermine shot through onto the cobbles. Outside it had finally started to pour with rain.

Radish galloped after her, a diamond tiara attached rakishly to his ears.

The nosebag swung from his bridle, jingling with swag.

"Get that **weasel**, Radish!" snarled Beef Wellington from the saddle.

Ermine stopped dead in her tracks. She removed the ruby from her teeth and turned to face them.

"I am <u>not</u> a weasel, I'm a **STOAT!**" she cried haughtily. "And you shouldn't be stealing other people's treasure! Minty – let them have it!"

Ermine leaped out of the way.

Minty squeezed the bubble-bath bottle as hard as she could.

Its **bubblicious** contents squirted in a great arc onto the rain-soaked cobbles.

Radish's hooves slithered and slid.

Beef Wellington tried to pull him up, but it was no good. The courtyard was as slippery as an ice rink! Horse and rider skated rapidly across it.

CRASH!

Beef Wellington and Radish crashed into a pile of old rubbish bags.

CLONK!

The swag bag fell at Minty's feet.

ZIP!

The tiara flew off Radish's ears and landed on Ermine's head.

Minty rushed over to where Ermine
still stood holding the dazzling ruby.
"WE DID IT, ERMINE!" she cried,
scooping Ermine up and giving her a
HUGE hug. "HOORAY!"

Beef Wellington pulled a banana skin off his head. "I'll get you for this!" he snarled.

The sound of sirens came from nearby. The police were on their way.

"No you won't," said Minty. "You'll end up in **prison** where you belong, like your ancestor William."

"Whereas Minty and I will go down in history as the **BRILLIANT detectives** who solved the mystery of the missing **Lambchop treasure**," said Ermine happily.

Radish bared his teeth.

Ermine paid no attention. She'd had enough of Radish and his funny faces. Instead she retrieved her Polaroid from Minty's backpack and pointed it at where the baddies lay in a **smelly** heap.

"Do you mind if Minty takes a photo for my scrapbook?" she said. "Only the Duchess said I had to fill it up!"

Dear Duchess,

Minty and I have been learning all about the Tudors. We've visited lots of palaces and I've met some very interesting people, including the Archbishop of Canterbury, the children from the Lambeth schools jazz band and the Kennington Tandoori tug-of-war team, not to mention Greville the beefeater. We also managed to solve the mystery of the Great Pastry Plot and recover the long-lost Lambchop ruby. It turned out Lord William Wellington hid it in the Crown Jewels! (Great detectives like Minty and I call that hiding something in plain sight, which is what I did by pretending to be an ermine collar, but that's another story.)

Anyway, luckily we managed to stop Wellington's rascally descendant from stealing everything. When Her Majesty, the present Queen, found out what happened, she said she'd like to keep all the jewels at the Tower for people to look at, if that was all right with us, and give Lord Lambchop some money to help save the jungle cats. We said that was fine, but we'd like to be part of history, and Her Majesty said we already were, and that she'd make sure all the guidebooks about London have me and Minty in them from now on. She has also invited Minty and me to afternoon tea at Buckingham Palace to say thank you. I shall definitely be taking my feathered hat!

Ermine xx

Grand Duchess Maria Von Schnitzel

The Imperial House of Hasbeen

Hasbeen Castle

Balaclavia

Europe

Ermine's Top Tips

London was first built nearly 2,000 years ago, when the Roman army invaded Britain. They built a town beside the River Thames, and named it Londinium. Nowadays, as Ermine and Minty discover, London is filled to the brim with things to see and do. Here are Ermine's top tips for sightseeing in the city!

Marvel at the Crown Jewels

Ever wanted to see the crowns and jewels that British kings and queens have worn for the past 600 years? Then head to the Tower of London! And, not just that, but you can also visit the prison that housed lots of historical prisoners, including Henry VIII's wife, Anne Boleyn. Can you spot a Beefeater and a raven while you're there?

Travel in style on a river cruise!

Like Ermine and Minty, you can jump aboard a boat to take in the sights of London by water... With routes from Putney to Greenwich and Richmond to Hampton Court, you can travel the River Thames like a Tudor monarch.

for Visiting London

Get lost in the Hampton Court Palace maze

And where better to end up than the Hampton Court Palace maze? The maze is legendary for bamboozling visitors with its twists and turns. It's the oldest surviving maze in the whole of England! Can you puzzle your way to the middle? (But watch out for those bees!)

Discover what Shakespeare's London might have felt like at the Globe

Ever wondered what it might have been like to go to the theatre in Tudor times? At the Globe, you can jump into the past and see where Shakespeare's plays were first performed. Wow!

Take to the skies on the London Eye!

And for something more modern, you can ride the ENORMOUS Ferris wheel on London's Southbank! Can you spot all the sights that Ermine and Minty visit from the sky?

To Flora, for accompanying me to the Lambeth Palace Gardens Fete and to Alice, for being incredibly determined. Jennifer

To Nicolò, for a new life in the UK together with our five pets. Elisa

First published in the UK in 2019 by Usborne Publishing Ltd., Usborne House, 83-85 Saffron Hill, London EC1N 8RT, England. www.usborne.com

Text copyright © Jennifer Gray, 2019
The right of Jennifer Gray to be identified as the author of this work has been asserted by her in accordance with the Copyright, Designs and Patents Act, 1988.

Illustrations copyright © Usborne Publishing Ltd., 2019
Illustrations by Elisa Paganelli.

The name Usborne and the devices 🔱🌐 are Trade Marks of Usborne Publishing Ltd.

All rights reserved. No part of this publication may be reproduced, stored in a retrieval system or transmitted in any form or by any means, electronic, mechanical, photocopying, recording or otherwise without the prior permission of the publisher. This is a work of fiction. The characters, incidents, and dialogues are products of the author's imagination and are not to be construed as real. Any resemblance to actual events or persons, living or dead, is entirely coincidental.

A CIP catalogue record for this book is available from the British Library.

JFM MJJASOND/19

ISBN 9781474964364 05323/1
Printed in the UK.